A Mail-Order Bride for the Shopkeeper

Brides of Leadville, Volume 1

Rhiana Rhiley

Published by Kayler Rose Publishing, LLC, 2024.

Table of Contents

Cover Design: Melba Moon
Pictures: depositphotos
Editor: Mary Marvella Barfield

This book is dedicated to my hardy pioneer ancestors who made Leadville their home.

Special thanks to my writing peeps at OIWi - Melba, Mary, Nanci, and Carol. Love you girls!

CHAPTER 1

Fall 1879

Addie Montgomery stared at her stepmother in shock. "My father wants me to leave?" Under normal circumstances, she would have found that hard to believe since her father had always told her she was welcome to continue living in their family home until she found her true love, even though she was already considered a spinster at twenty-two. But her father wasn't the same man he used to be. Since her mother's death eight months ago, he had acted withdrawn. He didn't seem to want anything to do with her anymore.

That, in and of itself, had shocked her, but even more shocking had been the day six months ago when he'd married their longtime housekeeper, Esther Cabot. After that, he completely stopped being the loving father he had always been.

After all of that, it wasn't so hard to believe her father wanted her to leave.

Esther gave her a look that said she felt sympathetic, but Addie knew that was far from the truth. As soon as Esther married Addie's father, the housekeeper seemed to hate Addie and treated her horribly. Her father either hadn't noticed or didn't care, and either way, it hurt.

In a sugary voice, Esther said, "You know how hard your father has taken your mother's death. You look so much like her he just can't bear to have you near any longer. You don't show any interest in any of the men who come calling."

Knowing her father wanted her to leave because she resembled her mother made it all that much more painful. It was like losing her mother all over again, but she was losing her father, too. "Surely, he doesn't expect me to leave when winter is setting in. I could possibly leave in the spring." Her voice sounded small to her own ears.

Esther's mouth turned up at the corners in a sly sneer. "The sooner you can go, the better it will be for him."

Unshed Tears stung Addie's eyes as she nodded and turned to mount the stairs.

"I left a few newspapers in your room so you can start looking for somewhere to go."

Esther's voice followed Addie up the stairs, causing spikes of pain to gouge at her heart. She found the papers lying on her bed. There were several different newsprints with quite an assortment of cities represented but none from Chicago. It was obvious they didn't want her anywhere nearby.

Addie sorted through the pile. Philadelphia, New York, Boston, Kansas City, Denver. She had no idea where Esther had come up with them all. There was also information on trains and fares to each place there was a newspaper for. Her stepmother had been busy collecting all this information.

She settled on the bed and flipped through the papers. She had no idea how she was to buy a ticket to somewhere new, let alone buy food and pay for a place to live once she got there. She hoped her father would give her some money to start out with, but her stepmother hadn't mentioned anything about funds.

Her father gave her an allowance each month. As luck would have it, she hadn't spent the money he'd given her this past month, so at least she would have a little bit if he and Esther didn't offer her anymore.

The newsprint blurred before her eyes as the tears ran out in a torrent. *Whatever am I going to do?* She'd never lived anywhere but here at home with her parents. With her father being a successful banker, they were one of the well-off families in town, so she never had to think about supporting herself before. How could she do such a thing?

Just as she was wadding the Rocky Mountain News into a ball, an advertisement caught her eye. She smoothed the paper back out and found the ad. Excitement coursed through her as she read it.

Wife Wanted

Healthy young man wishes to find a young lady willing to be my wife. I live in a thriving city in the mountains of Colorado.

If you are a healthy young lady interested in a stable home and a man to take care of you, please reply. I will respond with more information about me and my home. You can then decide if you think my offer would be a good choice for you.

Mr. Boyd Larson
Leadville, Colorado

Addie reread the advertisement several more times. Her heart pounded. It was perfect! She wouldn't have to worry about how she would support herself, and she would have a home. Taking a seat at her writing desk, she took out a sheet of paper and dipped her pen in the inkwell.

My Dear Mr. Larson,

I am writing in response to your advertisement in the Rocky Mountain News. I am interested in learning more about you and the opportunity that you offer.
I look forward to hearing from you.

Miss Adeline Montgomery
Chicago, Illinois

After slipping the letter into an envelope and addressing it, Addie wondered what to do with it. It was getting late, and the mail had been

3

taken to town this morning. It would have to wait 'til tomorrow to be posted. She would rather have sent it today. She hated the delay of even one day but stood and started toward the door. The thought of leaving it on the tray in the hallway downstairs where they usually left outgoing mail made her hesitate. She didn't want to chance Esther snooping at it.

If she was going to have to leave her home, then she didn't plan on letting her father and Esther know where she went. She didn't see any sense in it. It was obvious he wouldn't be interested in visiting her if he couldn't bear to have her around any longer. It would be best to cut all ties completely. It would be easier for her, anyway.

After deciding that, she hurried to don her cloak and tucked the letter in the pocket so it couldn't be seen. She would post it herself. She hoped she wouldn't run into her father or Esther. She sneaked out of her room and down the hallway without a noise.

At the landing, she paused, listening for footsteps below. Not hearing any, she slipped down the stairs and out the front door. She sighed as she descended the steps. She was thankful when she made it without anyone seeing her.

The trip to town had to be quick. She would need to be back before supper, so Esther wouldn't miss her.

AFTER SHE POSTED HER letter, she checked the mail every day. As much as she dreaded leaving the only home she had ever known, she didn't enjoy looking at Esther's face during meals. She avoided the former housekeeper at all costs. Taking her meals in her room allowed her that much. She really didn't want to hear the phony woman pretend she cared. Her father didn't leave his room to see her or for her to tell him her plans. Of course, she didn't expect him to. Well, he wouldn't have to avoid moving around in his house with her gone.

Addie had been checking the mail tray as soon as the servant left the mail there for what seemed like an eternity before a response to her letter arrived. She snatched it up and ran up the stairs before Esther saw her. Sitting on her bed, she slit the envelope open with her ivory-handled letter opener. Her heart raced as she slipped the folded paper out and read the contents.

My Dear Miss Montgomery,

It was nice to hear from you. As I stated in my first letter, here is more information on me and my home. My name is Boyd Larson. I am a kind, church-going man 26 years old. I own a general store in Leadville, Colorado. Leadville is a mining town located in the mountains of Colorado.

My wife passed away last year, and I would like to find a gentle, kind-hearted woman willing to wed me and help me run my store. In return, I will provide food and shelter, as well as safety for her.

If you agree to this arrangement, I will send traveling money, a train ticket to Denver, and a stage ticket from there on to Leadville as the train has not arrived in our fair city as of yet.

I can give you some time to think it over and we can correspond in an effort to become better acquainted.

Respectfully Yours,

Mr. Boyd A. Larson
Leadville, Colorado

Addie reread the letter several times, letting it all soak in before taking out a sheet of paper, her pen, and an inkwell to reply. A tingle of excitement coursed through her as she wrote back accepting his offer to send the means for her to travel out to him. There was no need to think about it further. It was a sound plan to get away from here with a home to go to and the means to get there. He was sure to be a responsible man if he owned a store in town. She prayed that was true. She could ask around town before she actually married him.

Esther had said the sooner the better, and she asked Addie every day when she was planning on leaving. As Addie saw it, she couldn't afford to waste any more time getting to know him or finding someone else. Besides, how well could you really get to know someone through letters? It was best to get there as soon as possible so they could get to know each other in person. She would have the money she'd saved for backup if he turned out to be a scoundrel, so she could get away from there if need be.

She didn't plan on letting Esther know Mr. Larson sent her money and tickets to get away from here or that she had her own bit of money saved up. If Esther and her father were gracious enough to give her the funds to leave, then she would add that to her emergency nest egg. In her opinion, it was the least they could do since they were asking her to leave the only home she'd ever known.

CHAPTER 2

After what seemed like an interminable amount of time to Addie, the day finally came when she was to leave her home and head west to wed a stranger. The enormity of what she was about to do hit her as she packed her trunk and bag. She wouldn't be able to take all her things so she would have to leave them behind. She would probably never see her home or her father again.

Addie's chest tightened making it hard to breathe. *What if Mr. Larson turns out to be a beast?* Her heart beating out a fast tempo, she clenched her fists. She couldn't go. She couldn't leave her home and her father.

She couldn't travel alone to a far-off land full of wild Indians and who knew what other kinds of dangers. She didn't know what she'd been thinking. A gracious letter explaining to Mr. Larson that she wouldn't be able to come after all should work fine.

When a shadow filled her doorway, she looked up to find Esther filling the opening with her plump figure. Her arms were crossed over her ample chest. Her eyebrows furrowed, and she had a pinched look on her face.

"Are you ready to leave? The train won't wait for you, you know." Her voice was cold.

Addie swallowed all her fears and misgivings. She had no choice but to leave. She stood. "Yes. I just finished packing. Please tell the servants they can load my things in the carriage. I want to say goodbye to my father, and then I'll be there."

"I'm not your servant. You can tell them yourself. Besides, your father is in his study and doesn't wish to be disturbed."

Addie bit back the rude reply she had on her tongue and instead said, "I'm sure he will come out to tell me goodbye."

"Has your father been out to say two words to you lately?"

Addie's heart felt as if it had fallen to the deepest pit of her stomach and lodged there. Her father had hardly been out of his study for months. He hadn't said anything to her since the day he'd announced his intention to wed Esther.

A sly smile curved Esther's lips, making her resemble an evil-looking Jack-o'-lantern. Her voice was laced with false sweetness. "Your father would rather not tell you goodbye. You understand..."

Deflated, Addie fought back tears. No, she didn't understand. She would never understand. She nodded though, refusing to cry in front of Esther. She grabbed her small travel bag and headed down the stairs and out the door to a new life.

ADDIE TRIED TO SHIFT into a more comfortable position on the hard seat of the stagecoach. Accustomed to riding in her father's luxurious personal train car, the trip in a regular coach car had been anything but luxurious. With each mile, she wished she had planned her trip more carefully and brought something to eat. None of the passengers in her car showed any interest in conversation to make the time pass more quickly.

It had been warm during the day and cold at night. She wasn't accustomed to sleeping sitting up but had managed to somehow.

The train had been the lap of luxury compared to the stagecoach. It was more like riding crammed in the baggage car with all the bags the way everyone was packed onto the hard seats. Her father's buggy would have been more comfortable. The air was dusty and nearly impossible to breathe at times. Addie didn't know how the driver could stand it. She was hardly able to sleep with all the jostling the coach did as it traversed the rugged mountain road. When the stagecoach driver announced Leadville was the next stop, she felt relief, fear, and excitement, all at once.

Addie's legs were so shaky from the rough ride she wondered if they were going to hold her when she stood. She was relieved when they did as she stepped down off the stagecoach at the stage station.

She gazed around and sucked in a breath at the view. Enormous mountains surrounded the town. She'd never seen anything like them. Their snow-covered peaks rose up to the robin-egg blue sky. The very topmost peaks were enveloped in puffy white clouds. Addie simply stood and stared at the beautiful sight, so all else around her dimmed into the background.

She stood admiring the view a few moments before she realized someone was calling her name.

"Miss Montgomery?"

When she turned, she spotted a tall man standing further down the platform waving at her. He was so tall that he stood well above the other people who were scrambling about on the platform.

When she waved back to acknowledge him, he started towards her. As he wound his way through the throng of people, she took in his appearance. As well as being quite tall, he had broad shoulders, and his arms looked muscular through the white shirt he wore.

His hair was such a pale blonde that it was almost white and touched the top of his collar. When he got closer, she could see that his eyes were a bright arresting blue. He was so handsome it nearly took her breath away. She hadn't expected that.

The man came to a stop in front of her and held out a large hand. "Miss Montgomery? I'm Boyd Larson. I recognize you from your description."

Addie automatically placed her hand in his and managed to answer, even though her mind was having a hard time grasping that this handsome man was her intended. She'd been afraid he would be a short, pudgy, bald man. "Mr. Larson. It's a pleasure to meet you."

"The pleasure is all mine, I assure you."

A tingle raced up her arm as he pressed a kiss to the back of her hand. She stared at their hands a moment, not sure what had just happened. She raised her eyes, and the instant they met his, she was lost in their blue depths.

CHAPTER 3

A zing of pleasure shot through Boyd when he kissed his intended bride's hand. He fought to push it away. She was breathtaking with her fiery red hair coming loose from its pins and trailing down her back.

He had thought someone desperate enough to answer a mail-order bride ad would be plain and unappealing. He had counted on it so that he wouldn't be attracted to her. He didn't understand why someone as beautiful as Miss Montgomery would need to answer an ad for a wife.

It was impossible to look away when their eyes met. The emerald green of her eyes was striking against her pale skin and the freckles that were scattered lightly across her nose.

The contact was finally broken when she looked down as if embarrassed. He didn't know what to make of his own reaction to her. He couldn't allow himself to develop feelings for her. He hoped it was just desire that drew him to her and not anything more. He hadn't recovered from the loss of his wife.

"I'm sure you've had a long, dusty trip on the stage. I know what a rough ride it can be. I've got a room ready for you in our apartment if you need to clean up or rest. We also have a fine restaurant and a café if you're hungry."

Addie's eyes lit up, and she smiled at that suggestion, sending desire shooting through Boyd.

"It has been quite a while since we dined last. A hot meal sounds wonderful. A bath and a nap in a real bed afterward would be absolute heaven."

"I'll have the porter take your bags to the apartment." He held out his arm for her. A tingle raced up it when she laced hers through it. He shook his head. He should have made it plain in his ad that he didn't want a raving beauty to reply. She didn't look like she would be able to endure the harsh climate that the high altitude of Leadville provided.

The desire he felt for her worried him. As long as he could keep his heart out of it, he would be fine. The thought that he should send her back at once so he wouldn't become attached to her gnawed at him as they walked to the hotel. He decided it would be best to talk to her about sending her home as soon as she ate and had some rest.

They ate a delicious meal of roasted pheasant with potatoes and carrots, as well as a moist chocolate cake with creamy chocolate frosting. They washed it all down with a glass of fresh milk.

Boyd leaned back in his chair, fully satisfied with his meal. The cook employed at the hotel's restaurant did a fine job. It didn't make up for having a wife who cooked for him, though.

He glanced over at Miss Montgomery and wondered if she could even cook. She looked more like she was used to having servants wait on her than doing anything for herself. He did have to admit that she was enjoyable company. She was also way too pretty and desirable for his peace of mind.

Hands steepled on the table in front of him, he looked over the top of them at her as she ate the last bite of her cake. Her small pink tongue licked the frosting off her lip, drawing his eyes to it. The sight of it fired his desire for her even more. He shifted in his chair and forced his mind to other things.

"So, tell me, Miss Montgomery, how are your cooking skills?" Her blush in response made him think he must have been correct in his earlier assumption that she couldn't cook. Her words somewhat belied that though.

"I'm afraid they're not very good yet. We had a cook most of my life. My stepmother only recently started teaching me how to cook a few months ago. I wasn't able to get much practice in before it was time to leave."

"I see." He wondered what had changed in their lives that made it necessary for her to learn to cook instead of their still keeping a cook as they were used to.

"And what about housekeeping skills?"

She lowered her head. "I'm afraid I only just recently started learning those also. You see, our cook was also our housekeeper."

"I see." He sighed as dismay ran through him. So, she was a pampered rich girl. Well, she had been learning those skills *recently,* as she put it. Everyone had to start somewhere. He just hoped helping him run the store wouldn't be too much for her.

The thought of sending her back ran through his mind again. "Well...I was hoping to have found someone with more experience than that in domestic duties. I'm not sure you will be able to handle the work. Perhaps, it would be better if I bought you a return ticket to Chicago after you rest a few days."

Her head snapped up, and her eyes were wide. "Please, Mr. Larson, don't send me back to Chicago. I have no home there to return to."

Again, he wondered what had happened to change her situation in Chicago. Her father must have lost his fortune if they had to give up their hired help and no longer had a home. Well, that decided it for him. He couldn't send anyone homeless and penniless back to such a sad situation. What would become of her?

He reached across the table and squeezed her hand. "Don't fret over it. We'll make it work." He hoped what he said was true. If she couldn't handle the store duties, he wasn't sure how they could make it work.

Relief showed in her eyes. "Thank you. I promise I'll learn to be a good wife for you."

Boyd gave her a tight smile in return, trying to push away the feeling that he was making a big mistake by letting her stay. He stood and held out his hand to her. "Are you ready to see our apartment? I'll heat some water and bring it in for you to bathe."

Addie returned his smile and took his hand, causing flames to shoot up his arm. "That would be wonderful."

When they reached the store, he opened the door for her and ushered her through. Once inside, he led her through to a curtained doorway that opened into an office and to the staircase at the rear of the room.

They climbed the stairs. At the top, Boyd opened the door to a small apartment. "I'll heat some water and tote the tub in so you can take a bath."

Once the copper tub was sitting in the middle of Addie's room and filled with hot water, Boyd said, "I'll leave you to it. After you're finished, if you feel like it, come on down and I'll show you around. Otherwise, I can show you around later if you need to rest first."

"Thank you, Mr. Larson. I will most likely take you up on your offer of rest before getting oriented with the store."

"I've closed the store for a few days so we can get to know one another, and we aren't open on Sundays, so you have a few days to rest before the store opens again. Just let me know if you need anything."

For some strange reason, he was reluctant to leave. He forced himself to turn and walk away, closing the door after himself. He strode down the hall toward the stairs, wondering what was wrong with him. Perhaps he was coming down with something. He raised a hand to his forehead. He didn't feel hot.

He shook his head in confusion as he descended the stairs and went to his office. Even his late wife Mary hadn't caused such a reaction in him. It wasn't right that this new woman should, especially so soon after he'd met her. Guilt over his desire for someone other than Mary assailed him, so he forced his mind off the beautiful Miss Montgomery.

After taking a seat at his desk, he pulled out his business ledger and went to work on the numbers. It was a mundane task that should keep him from thinking about his wife-to-be upstairs, soaking in the tub naked. He shifted in his seat as desire flared through him with that thought.

CHAPTER 4

S lamming the ledger closed and standing, he strode out of the office, intent on finding something around the store that would keep him busy enough not to think about her.

When he couldn't find any tasks that needed his immediate attention, he headed outside. A walk around town would surely clear his head. Then he could get back and concentrate on his ledger. He was behind in his accounting and needed to make recent entries in it.

As he stepped out into the bright sunshine, he noticed one of his good friends coming out of the hotel across the road. He raised his hand in greeting and crossed over to speak with him.

"It's good to see you, Lucas."

"Boyd, I hear your bride arrived this afternoon," his friend greeted him.

A groan slipped out before Boyd could stop it. Here he was trying to stop thinking about the woman, and his friend brought her up first thing.

"That bad, huh?" Lucas frowned at him.

"Well, that would depend on how you define *bad*. She happens to be a beautiful woman who is upstairs in her room taking a bath. That fact has caused me to be out here trying to cool off."

Lucas grinned. "Ahhh. I see. She's gorgeous, and it has you all stirred up, but you don't want that."

Boyd shook his head. "Of course not. I loved Mary. I was hoping for a plain woman so I wouldn't have to deal with any desire for her."

Lucas laughed. "You are in a pickle, aren't you?"

"I don't find any humor in it at all. I don't want to be unfaithful to Mary." He looked down at the ground.

His friend's voice sobered. "Mary is dead, Boyd. You need to accept that and get on with your life. She wouldn't want you to live in a loveless marriage. She'd want you to fall in love again and be happy."

Boyd's head shot up. "Well, I may not be able to live in a marriage without the husbandly benefits, but I'm not about to fall in love with anyone else."

"Think about what I said. I've got to get back in the hotel," Lucas said. His friend gave him a pat on the back before he headed back across the street.

"As if I can think about anything else after meeting Miss Montgomery," Boyd said under his breath so Lucas couldn't hear him. He had no idea how to resolve this problem. It hadn't even occurred to him that his bride-to-be would turn out to be so beautiful.

While he was deep in thought, his feet carried him further down the boardwalk and away from his intended.

"Howdy, Boyd."

He turned to find he'd passed the Assayer's office and the owner who stood outside the door calling to him. He lifted his hand in greeting to his buddy.

"I heard your bride came in on the afternoon stage."

"Howdy, Quinton. News sure travels fast around here." Annoyed that Miss Montgomery was the topic of everyone's conversation today, his voice came out gruffer than he intended.

"Well, what's she like?"

"She is a beautiful woman who was apparently pampered her whole life," he said, trying to stay focused on the one thing that he didn't find attractive about her.

Quint laughed. "Well, it won't take long around here for her to learn how to get along without all that pampering."

He grimaced. "That's one of the things that worries me. What if she decides she can't live without it all and wants to return home? I already gave her the option of returning home immediately."

"Ouch. That seems awfully cold to send her back right away just because of that. What was her reaction to that?"

"Well, that's not the only reason I want to send her back. She can't even cook." His excuses sounded petty even to his ears.

"I'm sure she will learn everything she needs to in time. Is she a shrew?"

Boyd shook his head.

"What else could be wrong with her then? You already said she's beautiful."

Boyd shifted uncomfortably. "That is probably the biggest problem and the fact that she appears to be a very nice lady and intelligent, too."

Quinton shook his head. "I don't see what the problem is then. Did you want someone who wasn't very bright?"

He thrust his hands into his pockets and shrugged. "No, that's not it at all."

His friend raised an eyebrow. "You didn't want her to be beautiful?"

"It would have been easier if she weren't."

"What exactly are you afraid of?"

"I'm not afraid of anything," he said with a touch of defensiveness in his tone.

"Well, it's mighty strange that you'd want an ugly bride to show up. I'd better get back into work." Still chuckling, Quint turned back to enter his office.

Boyd walked back toward the store, wondering if he was being ridiculous. He really was quite fortunate that his bride didn't turn out to be an ugly shrew, but the fact that she hadn't turned his insides to jelly and messed with his equilibrium in a way he had never experienced before. He didn't know if he could handle it and remain immune to her.

Entering the apartment, he noted that the tub had been removed from her room and was back in its usual place next to the stove in the kitchen. He had an urge to go in and check on Miss Montgomery, but he resisted it and headed back downstairs to his office. She was tired and needed a rest. He didn't need to bother her now.

Frustrated that he couldn't get her out of his mind and yearned to see her again already, Boyd poured himself into the bookwork that he needed to get done.

WHEN SUPPERTIME CAME and his intended still hadn't made an appearance downstairs, he decided he should check on her. It was against his better judgment to seek out her company, but he couldn't very well leave her up there alone if she were ill or something. She'd had a long journey, and it could have taken a toll on such a pampered creature.

Boyd took the stairs two at a time in his haste to ensure that all was well with her and stopped in front of her room. His palms were sweaty, so he wiped them up and down his pant legs a few times. He took a deep breath for courage and tapped on her door, in case she was still sleeping.

He sucked in a breath when she opened the door a few moments later wearing a dressing gown, her hair rumpled from her nap.

She blushed a pretty pink and pulled her gown closer together.

"I'm sorry I woke you. I thought you'd be awake by now. It's past suppertime."

Her hand flew to her mouth. "Oh my, I didn't realize I'd slept so long. Forgive me."

He looked down at his feet. "Nothing for me to forgive." *Why is she apologizing?* Mary would have berated him for waking her.

"If you'll excuse me, I will don my gown and join you."

At his nod, she shut the door on him. He paced up and down the hall a few times, then giving that up, he leaned back against the wall. He just wasn't sure what to make of Miss Montgomery or his body's reaction to her.

Addie rejoined him a few minutes later, wearing a different gown than the one she'd arrived in. "I'm sorry to have kept you waiting, Mr. Larson."

"If we are to be married, you should call me Boyd."

A blush infused her cheeks as she said, "Alright, Boyd."

The way she said his name sent a shaft of desire through him. Maybe he shouldn't have told her to call him by his first name. He hadn't reacted so acutely when she'd addressed him formally. He stamped his desire down. "Is it alright if I call you Adeline?"

Her blush darkened. "I prefer to go by Addie."

"Addie it is." He held his arm out for her. "Shall we head to the café?"

She nodded and slipped her arm through his, causing his desire to flare again. *How am I ever going to survive this?*

CHAPTER 5

The bath and nap had done wonders for Addie, and her mood was much improved. Ravenous, she ordered the same meal Boyd ordered, a T-bone steak, baked potato, and steamed vegetables. He raised an eyebrow at her as his eyes wandered over her.

"Pretty big meal for such a little thing." His voice held a hint of laughter.

Warmth suffused her face. "I'm awfully hungry after my rest."

He smiled. "Well, it's a choice I highly recommend. You look much better after your nap, more color in your face."

"I feel so much better after that long trip. I just wish I hadn't slept so long. I would have loved to have a tour of the town."

"No need to fret. We have plenty of time for it. How about I take you and show you around tomorrow if the weather holds?"

She smiled. "That would be wonderful. I didn't see much when I arrived, plus I was so tired. It looks like a nice place. I'm anxious to see more of it."

"I'll rent a carriage, and we can tour the town. We can even go for a ride to see the outlying beauty."

Addie clapped her hands in excitement. "Oh Boyd, that sounds wonderful."

She thought he looked like he reddened a bit when he said, "Consider it done. I'll arrange it all after supper."

Their meal arrived, and they were silent for several minutes as they dived into their dinners.

"I can show you around the store when we finish eating, if you like."

Between bites, Addie said, "I would like that."

Unsure what else to talk to her intended husband about, Addie remained silent as she finished her meal. He was already done and sat back in his chair to watch her, making her self-conscious as she ate. She wasn't sure why it bothered her so. She had impeccable manners since she'd been taught by a governess her father had employed.

That was before he had hired Esther as their housekeeper and cook. It seemed as if times had been more carefree before Esther had entered their lives, even when her mother was still alive. She shook that glum thought away, determined not to let thoughts of Esther intrude on the delicious dinner she was enjoying with her handsome betrothed.

Worry had gnawed at her the entire trip to Leadville. She'd been so afraid he would turn out to be some dirty old man or worse, someone who would be cruel to her. Esther had been sure to tell her all about men who were like that...nice one minute and mean the next.

Boyd seemed like a true gentleman, though, and he was so handsome it stole her breath away. She was lost every time she gazed into the deep blue of his eyes. The dimples that appeared when he smiled gave him a boyish appearance that was hard to resist.

She'd never dreamed he would be so handsome or so nice. She wasn't quite sure how to deal with him. Whenever he touched her, tingles shot up her arm, and a funny fluttery feeling invaded her stomach.

Esther hadn't mentioned anything about such things to her, so she was pretty sure it must be something good that was happening between them and not something bad. Esther had thrived on telling her about anything horrible that could happen with her betrothed and had never told her anything good that could possibly happen. Surely, it wasn't all bad. Otherwise, she didn't understand why people would marry at all.

Even though the feelings he invoked in her frightened her, they also thrilled her and gave her hope that somehow everything would work out fine between her and Boyd.

Once they were finished with their meal, Boyd took her for a tour through the store as promised. They ended it back in the office near the stairway that led to the rooms above.

"So, you live here above the store, Boyd?" Addie still felt shy about addressing him by his first name.

"There's another room in the apartment that I use."

"You didn't show me that."

He smiled, his dimples begging her to caress them. "No, I didn't. You get to see that once we're married."

"Oh, that's enticing. Perhaps we should proceed with our marriage tomorrow," she said, feeling reckless. *What does it matter if we know each other better or not?* She knew enough about him to know that he was an honorable man. She wasn't afraid of him and believed he would never hurt her.

He raised his brows at her. "Is that really what you'd like to do?"

With a nod, she laid her hand on his arm. "We'll have the rest of our lives to get to know each other." She thought the look that crossed his face looked like fear but decided it must be nerves. After all, he was the one who had advertised for a bride and asked *her* to come out west to marry him. Besides, he had already been married once. He certainly couldn't be afraid of marriage.

She gave his arm a squeeze, feeling the muscles beneath his sleeve. Warmth suffused her, and she had a sudden urge to feel more than just his forearm. She looked up at him in confusion, wondering what was happening to her and why he was having this effect on her.

Looking uncomfortable, Boyd shifted and stepped away from her. Addie dropped her hand, disappointment flowing through her. He acted as if he didn't like having her touch him, not at all like he was having the same reaction she was.

His reaction disturbed her almost as much as her reaction to him did. She gave her head a shake, trying to sort out her confusing thoughts and feelings.

Embarrassed by both her reaction to him and his to her, she turned toward the staircase. "It's been a long day. I think I'll turn in."

She grasped the wooden railing and started up the stairs. Suddenly, Boyd was by her side with his hand on her elbow.

"I'll walk you to your room."

She stopped and turned to him. "That's really not necessary."

He smiled, making his alluring dimples stand out on his handsome face. "I insist."

With a shrug, she resumed walking.

At her door, he took her hand and gave it a squeeze. "Goodnight, Adeline."

Tingles ran up her arm from where his warm hand touched hers. Disturbed by her reaction, she pulled her hand loose and escaped into the room without a word. *How can my feelings be hurt by his reaction one second and in the next second change to me wanting to throw myself into his arms?* It made no sense at all to her.

CHAPTER 6

The next morning, Boyd took Addie to the local café for breakfast. She was self-conscious over her actions the night before and his reaction to her. She was quiet during breakfast and only picked at her food. Though Esther had told her several times about how ugly she was, she hadn't realized she was so ugly that her intended husband wouldn't be able to stand her.

It was quite apparent he didn't want to marry her. He'd tried to send her back home almost as soon as he had laid eyes on her. Esther must have been right. Her flaming red hair and bright green eyes must be repelling to men or at least to one man in particular. Her betrothed certainly must feel that way about her.

Unsure what she would do if Boyd ended up sending her back to Chicago, an unusual melancholy settled over Addie. She put down her fork, all pretense of eating gone with that thought. She stared down at her plate in despair. She couldn't go home. Her father and Esther didn't want her there any more than Boyd apparently wanted her here with him.

"Are you alright, Addie?" He put his hand on her arm.

She raised her head to look at him, unbidden tears filling her eyes. "I don't know what to do if you want to send me home. I'm...I'm not welcome there any longer."

Boyd frowned at her. "What do you mean, you're not welcome there?"

"My father doesn't want me there."

"He told you that?" His voice sounded incredulous.

"No, Esther told me."

"And who is Esther?"

"She's my stepmother. She used to be our housekeeper before my mother passed away." She took a deep breath to try to control her tears. "After my mother died, my father married her rather suddenly. Everything changed after that."

"So, your stepmother told you she didn't want you there and your father didn't say otherwise?"

Addie wiped at her tears. "No, she told me my father no longer wanted me there. He had taken to locking himself in his study and seldom spoke to me anymore."

Boyd pulled her into his arms. "I'm sorry that happened. Now I understand why you chose to answer my letter. I won't send you back. We'll work it out."

The warmth of his arms helped calm Addie's fears. *How could I break down in front of him like this?* She should pull away, but she couldn't bring herself to. It felt so good to be wrapped in his strong arms. She wondered what it would be like to be his wife, to always feel this way.

She felt safe and protected, and though he hadn't said he wanted her here with him, at least he wasn't going to send her back. They would work something out. She wondered what kind of arrangement they would work out. He didn't seem to want her for his wife.

Maybe she could at least help him run the store. It would provide her with an income and maybe a place to live. It was better than returning home where she wasn't wanted at all.

After a few minutes, he pulled away from her. "Are you okay?"

With a sniff and a dab at her eyes to dry them, she nodded.

"Are ready for your tour of Leadville then?"

She straightened her shoulders and smiled shyly. "Whenever you are."

He held out his arm to her. "Then let's go."

They exited the store and stepped out onto the boardwalk. The boardwalk was crowded with people, but not as crowded as the street. There were wagons, coaches, horses, and people moving down the street.

It was packed from one side to the other with the congestion clogging the streets.

"There are so many people. I didn't realize it was such a large metropolis." Addie could hear the awe in her own voice.

It wasn't like back home in Chicago, though. Where she had lived, there were fine carriages with well-dressed men and women.

Here, there were wagonloads of settlers. There were also rough-looking men on horses or mules, some even on foot.

"It's growing fast. Many men seeking their fortunes in the mines come here at some point. A lot of them uproot their families and bring them along."

"So, the mining is what's bringing them all?"

"Most of 'em. Everybody thinks they're going to strike it rich. I hear we're getting close to 30,000 people. We have three newspapers."

"Oh my, I had no idea. What is it they mine?"

"Well, it started as a gold rush in the 60s, but that dried up, and it became a silver rush in '77."

The boardwalk was crowded, but they were able to make their way down it. Boyd pointed out the sights to her as they went.

"That's the new Tabor Opera House. It's supposed to open later this month." He pointed to a large new building that was under construction. It was tall and had awnings over the lower front windows.

"Oh, I've heard of Horace Tabor and how he struck it rich out west. I didn't realize it was here. That's a beautiful building."

"The inside is said to be spectacular. Would you like to attend a show there sometime?"

Addie smiled in excitement. "I'd love to, especially now that you've got me interested in seeing the inside of the building."

"You've got a deal. I'll see about tickets soon as it opens."

"I didn't realize Leadville was so modern as to have an opera house."

Boyd smiled. "It's all the money from the men who have struck it rich. They want a town that will rival any city back east. We have a police and fire department. Our fair city even has telephone and water. Gas illumination installation will be finished later this month. I thought about getting water and gas installed in our apartment but decided to save the money. I'd really like to build us a house of our own one day."

There was pride in his voice as he spoke about his community.

"I must say, it does make me feel better knowing it isn't as primitive as I thought it would be."

"That's St. Vincent's, our new hospital that opened last year. It's a very modern medical facility." He pointed out another new building in the distance.

"It's so beautiful here. The mountains are so huge. I feel like an ant looking up at them."

Boyd laughed. "They call it the Arkansas Valley because the Arkansas River flows through. Those mountains there are the Mosquito Mountains." He pointed to a mountain range in the distance.

He turned the other way and pointed to a large mountain. "That's Mount Elbert." He pointed in another direction where a large mountain loomed over the town. "That one is Mount Massive."

Growing up in the Midwest, Addie had never seen mountains like these before she came out West. "They're beautiful, but so large. I love their colorful names." She laughed.

They made their way across the street, taking care to avoid any wagons or horses, and started back towards the store.

"I will take you out for a ride to see the countryside as soon as I can arrange it."

"Oh, thank you, Boyd. And thank you for bringing me out here." *This feels like home already.* "It's so beautiful. I don't think I'd ever care to leave."

He smiled. "I'm glad you like it, Addie."

His boyish dimples took her breath away every time he smiled at her. Perhaps things would work out, after all. He really was a charming and handsome man. She'd be proud to be his wife. If only he felt the same about having her for his wife.

Time was all they needed, all he needed. Then he'd see that they could have a good marriage. Maybe they would even come to love each other someday. He wouldn't be a hard man to love. She was already quite taken by him. Something told her it wouldn't take her long to learn to love him.

CHAPTER 7

The next day, as promised, Boyd took her for a carriage ride through Leadville and then headed out of town. He explained they were going for a ride to show her the valley. It was a beautiful ride. The mountains stood sentinel around them, but the valley itself resembled a meadow with a forest surrounding it. The pine trees loomed above. The fragrance reminded Addie of Christmas.

When the sun was high in the sky, Boyd stopped under the shade of a tree at the edge of the meadow. To Addie's surprise, he pulled out a blanket and a picnic basket that she hadn't noticed. He climbed out and helped her down, then spread the blanket in the grass in the sun near the tree and placed the basket in the middle of the blanket.

"It's been surprisingly nice for this late in the season. We usually have snow by now," Boyd said.

Addie smiled at him as he held his hand out to her. "I had no idea you had all this planned."

"I had a picnic lunch prepared for us. I thought I'd surprise you."

A giggle escaped her. "I am surprised."

After taking a seat, she opened the basket and took out the contents. There was fried chicken and a bowl of potato salad, as well as rolls spread with fresh butter. There were dishes and silverware included.

"It looks delicious." She laid it all out.

They ate in silence for a few minutes. Addie watched Boyd while he ate a piece of chicken. He was so sweet to have surprised her with a picnic. She felt him take another piece of her heart along with him.

After finishing the chicken leg that he was eating, Boyd reached for another piece. His eyes met hers, and she felt herself drawn into the blue depths of his eyes. Just when she thought she was drowning in them, he broke the contact and looked down at his plate of food.

"I was thinking, if you still want to marry me, I'll talk to the preacher and see if we can do it Sunday after services."

His eyes met hers again, and an unexpected thrill raced through her. He still wanted to marry her. She tried to control the excitement in her voice as she said, "That would be lovely."

"Good, I'll go see the preacher as soon as I take you back to the apartment." He smiled at her, his dimples sending a tingle through her.

She couldn't wait to become Mrs. Boyd Larson. She would be proud to have him as her husband. Still, though, she warned herself to watch her emotions. Though he had asked her to marry him, she had no doubt that he didn't have any feelings for her. It was simply a business arrangement. She had to keep that in mind.

Clouds gathered over the mountain above them and let loose a shower of rain. It didn't come down as far as the valley where they sat, but Addie could tell it was raining on the mountain.

By the time they finished their picnic, a beautiful rainbow was shining across the valley with Mosquito Mountain in the background. The sight took Addie's breath away. She took it as a sign that things were going to work out for her and Boyd. After all, he had decided to go ahead and marry her. It was like nature was happy that he had decided that.

Boyd loaded everything back into the carriage and helped Addie up to the seat. She was surprised when he didn't head back to town like she thought he would. Instead, he kept going the way they had been heading. To her delight, he showed her more of the beautiful countryside before they returned to town late that afternoon.

After Boyd dropped Addie at the apartment, he went to return the carriage and seek out the preacher. Addie retired to her room where she spun in circles with her arms outstretched until she got too dizzy to continue. She was so happy she didn't think she could stand it.

Boyd wanted to go ahead and marry her, after all. She'd been so afraid he had changed his mind. She believed she could be happy being Boyd's wife. She also believed that he might be happy being her husband, given time.

Tired after all the excitement that day, she flopped down onto the bed and stared up at the ceiling. She had less than a week to prepare for her wedding. She had her mother's wedding dress tucked away in her cedar chest. Her mother had given it to her to keep in her hope chest until she needed it.

With a sigh of disappointment, Addie wished her mother could be there with her on her wedding day. She missed her terribly and could use some motherly advice right now about what to expect on her wedding night.

CHAPTER 8

The date was set for Sunday after services. Boyd felt uneasy after talking to the preacher. It was the right thing to do. He had sent for Addie to come here to be his wife. He couldn't back out now, knowing that she had no home to go back to.

It still worried him about marrying her though. He didn't want to fall in love with her, and he was afraid it might be hard to resist her. She was so beautiful and such a delight to be around. She pulled at his heartstrings without even trying. She would be irresistible if she tried to win him over. He didn't think he could withstand it and still come out with his heart intact.

There was nothing to do about it now. He would just have to try to harden his heart toward her or not spend much time with her. Otherwise, he wouldn't be able to resist her charms. His mind was in turmoil about it, so he took a leisurely route back to the hotel. He maneuvered around people and wagons to take a walk around town before he returned to his bride-to-be.

The clear mountain air helped clear his head so he could think better, and after his walk, he felt better about it all. He had made the right decision.

Since the store was still closed, it was quiet when he returned. After checking around, he found that Addie had retired to her room. It took some getting used to the high altitude and the thin mountain air in Leadville, so he didn't disturb her since she might be sleeping.

In all truth, he was relieved she wasn't available. He could use the time to catch up on his bookwork.

ONCE AGAIN, IT WAS well past suppertime when Boyd went up to check on Addie, since she'd never come down. He tapped on the door.

When there was no answer after several seconds, he rapped a little louder. "Addie, are you alright?"

A few seconds later a sleepy voice said. "What? Oh, yes. I'm fine. I'll be right out."

Her face was bright red when she appeared at the door a few minutes later. "I'm so sorry. It appears I fell asleep again while I was awaiting your return."

Boyd chuckled. "No need to apologize. You aren't used to this high altitude. It can make you sleepy at first."

She smiled somewhat shyly at him. "I thought you'd come up when you returned."

"I didn't want to disturb you."

"How did it go?" Her face reddened again.

"It was quite successful. Everything is set for Sunday after services." Excitement surged through his body when he told her the news. He didn't understand why he was so excited about it. He'd been dreading it ever since she arrived.

"I'm glad it worked out so well."

It made no sense to him at all when he had the sudden urge to pull her to him and kiss her in celebration. He tamped it down and refused to acknowledge it again. Although it would be nice to just sit and hold her warm body to his and inhale her sweet scent, he shoved that desire away, too. He could do all that once they were married on Sunday afternoon.

The conflicting path his emotions were taking had him reeling in confusion. *What is going on with me?*

The gentle touch of her hand on his arm brought him back to the moment at hand.

"Are you happy with the plans, Boyd?"

The feel of her warm hand made it hard to concentrate on what she was saying. When her question registered, he smiled down at her. "I am, Addie. I really am."

BY THE TIME SUNDAY came around, Boyd was having serious doubts about his sanity. He didn't know what had come over him the day he'd proposed to her and set up the wedding. Oh yes, he was still attracted to her and still eager to make her his wife. That was the reason he was doubting his sanity.

The feelings he had for Addie had only intensified over the last few days. He found himself wanting her more and more. He was quite eager for their wedding and subsequent wedding night. *Will she let me exert my husbandly rights?* He surely hoped so.

News of their upcoming nuptials spread through town faster than a wildfire. By the day of their wedding, the women of the town had organized a reception after the wedding. They had even gone so far as to prepare a meal for the party.

Boyd's palms were sweating as he waited at the end of the aisle for his bride to appear. Lucas stood next to him as his best man. He hadn't been sure whom to pick between Lucas and Quinton. Quint had made it easy on him when he chose to walk Addie down the aisle since her father wasn't there to do it.

There hadn't been time for Addie to get acquainted with many people, so she had asked the waitress from the café to be her bridesmaid. Sarah was a charming young woman. Addie had become friends with her in the few days she had been in town. Boyd was glad she had made a friend so fast.

When Addie walked down the aisle beside Quinton a few minutes later, Boyd sucked in his breath. She was stunning in the ivory gown that she wore. He couldn't take his eyes off her during the nuptials and almost missed answering when it was time for him to say I do.

He didn't miss when the preacher told him he could kiss the bride, though. He pulled her close and placed a gentle kiss on her lips. Desire flared through him, and he wanted to intensify the kiss, but he refrained since it was their first kiss, and they were in church in front of a crowd. He didn't want to frighten or embarrass his new bride.

It was all over and done in no time, and they were walking back down the aisle as husband and wife. The townspeople gathered around them outside the church, cheering and congratulating them.

The women of the town had a meal all set up in the basement of the church, so everyone followed Boyd and Addie downstairs for the reception.

They ate a fine lunch of pot roast and gravy with rolls dripping with butter, after which cake was served all around. As the meal wound down, the town band struck up a tune.

Boyd escorted Addie out onto the dance floor and held her close while they danced a waltz together. He savored the feel of her warm body so close to his.

When their dance was finished, the band moved on to a rousing song that had all the guests getting to their feet and joining in. The dancing and merriment continued for hours.

As the sun was setting behind the mountains, Boyd looked over at Addie. She looked exhausted. He'd better get his bride home before she was too tired to do anything but go to sleep.

He sidled up next to her where she was getting a cup of punch. "You look tuckered out. Are you ready to go home, Mrs. Larson?"

She looked up at him with relief on her face. "I am, Mr. Larson."

Everyone cheered after they made their goodbyes and headed outside to their carriage. Boyd helped his new wife up into the carriage, then he followed. Sitting close to her on the seat felt too natural. Once they were going down the road, he slipped his arm around her. She didn't complain. Instead, she rested her head on his shoulder.

By the time they reached the store, he noticed a difference in her breathing and realized she had fallen asleep. He pulled up in front of the building and looked down at her. *Should I rouse her or just carry her in and up to our room?* Earlier in the day, he'd taken Addie's things from the room she'd been staying in and put them in his room.

In the end, he didn't have the heart to wake her, so he gathered her up in his arms and carried her inside. Once upstairs and in their room, he gently laid her on the bed. He stood staring down at her, struck by her beauty as she slept peacefully. There was no way he could undress her and put a comfortable gown on her.

It was hard to believe he was married...again. Even though that's what he'd intended when he brought Addie here, it turned out to feel surreal. When Mary died, he thought he'd never marry again. It had been a hard decision to send for a wife. If she wasn't so beautiful, he would have married her the first day she arrived.

Now, he wasn't sure how he was going to handle being married to her and keep his heart intact. He had no idea why he had suddenly decided the other day to ask her to go ahead and become his wife. He had a feeling he just enjoyed torturing himself.

When he finally shed his clothes and climbed into bed next to her, she snuggled into him. He put his arm around her and pulled her close. He would have to be content tonight with just holding her.

Addie's arm moved up to rest on his chest, and he froze. It took several seconds of deep breathing before he got his desire under control. Even with her wedding gown on, he could feel the heat of her body and smell her fresh floral scent. He placed a gentle kiss on her forehead and lay there wide awake, reveling in the feel of her in his arms. She was now his wife. They had the rest of their lives together.

CHAPTER 9

The next morning, Addie awoke to find herself wrapped in Boyd's arms with her arm thrown across his chest. She had slept in her wedding dress with a nearly naked man, her husband. Heat flooded her face, and she lifted her head to peek at him, but he seemed to still be asleep.

After disengaging herself from him, she rose and retrieved her clothes from her trunk, which had been brought into Boyd's suite yesterday. When she removed her rumpled gown, she placed it carefully over a chair. She shivered from the cold as she dressed in a forest green calico print dress. By the time she finished buttoning her boots with the cold metal boot buttoner, her fingers were getting numb.

With a last look at Boyd's face, so relaxed in sleep, she shut the door behind her and sprinted down the stairs. Once in the kitchen, she lit the fire in the stove, glad that Boyd was in the habit of preparing it the evening before since she wouldn't have known how to do it herself. It was easy to strike a match and hold it to the paper and kindling to get it going.

Making a pot of coffee was a different story. Looking at the coffee pot, she wondered what the tin basket suspended on the long stick inside was for. She finally decided that must be where the coffee should go. Searching the cupboards, she found a bag of coffee beans and filled the little basket to the top.

After that, she placed the small lid that had come off the basket back on and took the pot to the sink to pump water out of the spicket. It took a few pumps before water spewed out and then finally came out in a nice stream. She filled the pot with water.

When she lowered the basket of coffee beans back into the pot, water gushed over the side, and she realized she shouldn't have filled the pot so full. She put the lid on the pot and placed it on the burner, then lit the burner under the pot.

Pleased with herself for that accomplishment, she dug through the cupboards and pantry to see what she could fix for breakfast. A sizzling sound a few minutes later alerted her to the fact that the coffee pot must still be too full of water. She turned to see water boiling out the spout and sizzling in the fire of the burner.

Without thinking, she grabbed the handle of the pot to dump some of the water out. The heat from the handle seared her hand, and she dropped the pot back onto the burner with a loud clatter, causing the coffeepot to rock precariously. She just managed to grab the dishtowel and steady the pot before it fell over. As it was, some of the water splashed over the edge of the spout onto the burner before she righted the pot.

Tossing down the towel, she went to the handpump and worked the handle until water flowed out the spout, then she put her hand under the cool water to soothe it where she'd burned it. She examined her hand after she dried it. It was bright red but didn't look like it would blister. She let out a sigh of relief.

There were some eggs she had spotted in the pantry just before she'd heard the coffee pot boiling over, so she went and grabbed those. She would make scrambled eggs and hotcakes. She'd seen Esther do it, and neither of them looked hard to make. She remembered the ingredients Esther had used but had no idea what amounts of each thing to use.

After some more searching, she found a cookbook and flipped through it until she found a hotcake recipe. She found all the ingredients in the pantry and a big bowl in the cupboard. She carefully measured each ingredient as she added them to the bowl. Once she had the batter mixed, she was feeling proud of the fact she'd mixed it up properly. Cooking didn't seem to be as hard as she'd always thought.

Another search of the cupboards brought up a cast iron frying pan and a griddle to cook the hotcakes on. After placing them on the burners, Addie broke eggs into the pan, finding it wasn't as easy to keep pieces of the shells out as Esther had made it look. Addie picked the shells out as best she could and stirred the eggs together. To the griddle, she added some lard and watched as it melted then poured some batter onto it.

Busy with the hotcakes, she forgot to stir the eggs, and when she did, the bottom was as brown as a tree trunk, but the top was still raw. She stirred them together and left them to cook longer as she went back to the hotcakes. The first few were burnt on the bottom by the time she flipped them, so she didn't let them cook long before she took them off and placed them on a plate.

Afraid the eggs would burn, she dished them up onto plates before adding more batter to the griddle. She had to throw those hotcakes out when she tried turning them too soon and ended up with a gloppy mess all over the griddle. After scraping off the burnt batter, she added more lard and then the batter. This time, she left them a bit longer than the last time but made sure not to leave them for as long as the first batch and she was quite pleased with the way those hotcakes turned out.

The door to the kitchen opening alerted her to Boyd's presence before he spoke. "Good morning."

Spatula in hand, she turned to him with a smile. "Good morning. You're just in time for breakfast."

He smiled at her, and the dimples in his cheeks caused a fluttering in her stomach. He was so handsome it took her breath away. It awed her that he was now her husband.

Her new husband took a seat at the table, and she turned back to the stove to fill his plate full of food and pour him a cup of coffee. She set the plate and cup down in front of him and went back to dish up her plate and pour her coffee.

As she sat down and took in the breakfast before her, she felt like crying. The eggs were dark and crusty instead of light and fluffy like they were supposed to be. The coffee, though plenty hot, looked like dirty water, and she was afraid it would taste just as bad.

Boyd never said a word and dug into his food with relish as if it were the best meal he'd ever eaten. His smile never faltered, even when he took a drink of the coffee.

The first bite of eggs she took made her choke, so she quickly took a sip of coffee to wash it down. The coffee was so awful she almost spat it out but somehow managed to swallow it.

Fighting tears, Addie cut into her hotcake to find that the outside was tough and hard, but gooey batter ran out of the middle.

Unable to control her tears any longer, they ran down her cheeks as she looked over at Boyd. His plate was empty, which made her cry even harder.

With a frown, he asked, "What's wrong?"

"You...you ate all your breakfast..." she sobbed.

His look turned to confusion. "Didn't you want me to?"

"It's awful...how could you stand to eat it?"

Boyd scooted his chair close to her and took her in his arms. "It wasn't that bad. Truly. You should try some of the things I've tried cooking for myself." He laughed and held her tighter. "I'll eat anything you cook for me, Addie."

Addie sniffed a few more times, enjoying the feeling of being in his arms. She would like to snuggle up, lay her head on his chest, and stay there forever.

All too soon, he pulled away and wiped at her tears with his handkerchief. "There now, there's no need to cry."

His tenderness almost unleashed another torrent of tears, but she managed to keep them from falling. Then he saw the red welt on her hand where she had burned it, and with utmost care, he kissed the wound. The tears did start to fall then.

"What happened to your hand, Addie?"

"I...I burned it earlier," she admitted with a sob.

Boyd got up and left the room. He returned moments later with a tin of salve and some gauze. With extreme tenderness, he lightly applied some of the salve to the wound and then wrapped it with the gauze. When he was finished, he placed another kiss on her bandaged palm.

"There, all finished. You'll have to be more careful. I don't want you getting hurt."

With that, he took his leave to go open the store, leaving her wiping at her tears and wondering how he could be so sweet after the mess she had made of his breakfast.

CHAPTER 10

The next few months flew by for Addie. She and Boyd had consecrated their marriage on the second night. She felt her face heat as she thought of all the wonderful things he did to her body. She had never known there was such pleasure in marriage. The nights were a dream come true for her.

When they were making love, she could believe he was starting to fall in love with her. The thought thrilled her, though she was afraid she was beginning to fall in love with him, too, and she was not quite sure how to handle that.

They settled into a companionable routine, both at home and working in the store together. She had caught on to all he had taught her, so she could help him out. They worked quite well together, which seemed to please him.

During the day, he spent most of his time keeping so busy in the store that he did not have much time to even speak to her, and it seemed to her as if he avoided her as much as possible. She was puzzled by his behavior and was afraid she had done something to displease him, but he assured her there was nothing wrong when she asked him about it.

The only time things seemed right was when they were making love at night. She sighed as she dusted the shelves in the front of the store.

Her eyes were drawn to the front window. Large white flakes of snow floated to the ground, adding to the large amount they had already received. Winter in the high mountain town had been late, but it had hit with a vengeance after Christmas.

Addie had never seen so much snow at one time, not even during the worst winters back home. There was so much snow that it was piling up taller than the building in places, and what they shoveled out of the road they used to make sledding hills for the few children in town.

The cold was almost unbearable when she had to go out in it. She had thought Chicago's winters were bad. She found winter lasted longer here in the mountains than it had back home, too. It was now almost the end of April, but the snow had not let up yet. Boyd assured her that spring was right around the corner, but she was finding it hard to believe with snow blanketing everything in sight.

After joining the sewing circle in town and working in the store, Addie had made a couple of friends and enjoyed their company, but she longed for her husband to warm up to her outside of the bedroom. She had been hoping for a marriage like her parents had had before her mother had died.

They had talked for long hours, discussing any topic from menial ones to important ones. They had been united in every way, and that is what Addie wanted from her marriage. She should have known better, since her parents' marriage had been a love match, unlike her marriage of convenience. Maybe if she worked harder to please her husband...

Boyd's aloofness during the day had her feeling lonely and wondering if this was all her marriage was going to be. *If this is what my marriage consists of, can I stand it for the rest of my life?* All she wanted was for her husband to want to spend time together, to be a partner in every way, and possibly to fall in love with her, the way she feared she had with him.

A man entered the store, interrupting her thoughts. He was short and stout. His suit and jaunty little hat looked out of place in the western town where most of the men were miners or cowboys.

Addie watched as he approached the counter and spoke with Boyd. She wondered if he was a city man come to seek his fortune in the rugged mountains surrounding Leadville. She had seen plenty of them pass through the store getting supplies for their mining expeditions before they headed out of town again.

She was surprised when their conversation did not last long, and the man readied to leave without making a purchase. As the man was turning to leave, he caught sight of Addie. He seemed to study her carefully as he made his way to the door and left. His appraisal of her left her feeling uncomfortable.

Setting down her feather duster, she was headed to Boyd to ask him what the man had wanted when Mrs. Dewberry entered the store and approached her.

By the time she had finished helping Mrs. Dewberry pick out fabric for a new dress, Boyd was busy with a customer, and then the store was so busy the rest of the afternoon that Addie soon forgot all about the mysterious man.

That evening, Addie was exhausted and after cleaning up supper dishes, she joined Boyd in the parlor of their apartment. She collapsed into the rocking chair and put her feet up on the stool that she had placed in front of it. Some evenings, she was just too tired to rock and needed to simply elevate her feet.

A glance at Boyd showed him dozing with the open Bible forgotten in his lap. Tired as she was, a small smile touched Addie's lips. It appeared her husband was just as bushed as she was.

CHAPTER 11

B oyd awoke sometime later to find Addie asleep in her rocking chair, her feet propped on her footstool. He sat and gazed at her, drinking in the sight of her beautiful face peaceful in slumber. With a pang, he knew he had already fallen in love with her, even though he had tried his best not to.

He thought back over the past few months and realized it had most likely happened the first time they had made love. That was when everything seemed to change. He'd tried ignoring her as best as he could during the day, but he couldn't resist taking her in his arms each night.

As he watched her sleep, he wondered how he could rectify the situation. After considerable thought on it, the only conclusion he could come up with was that he would need to pull away from her at night, as well as during the day. He didn't want to do that because he loved exploring her body each night, but he couldn't risk his heart getting hurt.

With that decision firmly made, he rose and took care of the fire before going to bed. Leaving her asleep in her chair in the parlor was the hardest thing he'd had to do in a long time, but he knew if he woke her to go to bed, he wouldn't be able to resist making love to her that night. It was best to start his new plan of action at once, or he might never do it.

Once in bed, his mind and body had a hard time ignoring the fact that his wife was in the other room and all he had to do was go wake her and he could make love to her. It was a long time before he finally relaxed enough to drift off to sleep.

THE NEXT MORNING WHEN Boyd awoke, he found Addie curled up in his arms with her head resting on his shoulder, the same as he had every other morning since their marriage. He wanted to stay in bed and enjoy the feel of her warm body snuggled close to his, but he forced himself to get up and start the day.

When Addie joined him in the kitchen, he immersed himself in the newspaper so he wouldn't have to make conversation with her. When he glanced at her, he noticed the hurt look in her eyes before she tried to cover it up. He tried to bury his guilty feelings as he shifted his attention back to the paper.

It wasn't that he wanted to hurt her, because seeing that look hurt in her eyes cut him to the quick, but he had to protect himself from getting hurt first. There was no way he could go through what he had gone through before when Mary died. He didn't think he could survive something like that again.

No, it was better to pull away and let her feelings be hurt for a short time than to endanger his emotions like that again. Besides, she would surely get over her hurt soon enough. Once he had hardened his heart back toward her and felt safe that the barricade would hold, only then would he resume making love to her at night.

As soon as Boyd finished breakfast, he took his leave with the excuse that he had to work on the books before he opened. At the store with the ledger open before him, he couldn't concentrate on the numbers, though. His mind returned again and again to the hurt look on Addie's face that morning.

The more he worried about the situation with her, the more he convinced himself he should have let the gentleman who inquired about her yesterday know that she was here. He wasn't sure why he had told the man that he had never heard of her. It had just come out when he opened his mouth.

Maybe it was because he wanted to protect her, although what exactly he wanted to protect her from, he wasn't sure. Perhaps it was because he was sure it was her father who had sent the detective looking for her, the same father who was supposed to have sent her away without a qualm because she reminded him too much of his dead wife, and that didn't sit well with him.

Now, he wondered if part of the reason he had said that to the detective was because he was already falling in love with her. He shoved that away as soon as the thought entered his head. He couldn't be falling in love with her already...he couldn't or shouldn't be falling in love with her at all.

It also occurred to him that perhaps her story about her father sending her away wasn't the truth, after all. But why would Addie make up such a story if it wasn't true? An awful thought took root in his head. Maybe she had made that story up because she had been afraid that he would send her back.

The thought that she had perhaps duped him didn't sit well with him. It might be wise for him to get in touch with that detective agency the man had said he was from and arrange to have her sent back to her father, after all. He didn't want a wife he couldn't trust.

CHAPTER 12

Addie had noticed the change in Boyd right away when she had awakened and found he had gone to bed without her. Normally, he would have awakened her, and they would have gone to bed together, making love before curling up together to sleep. She had made excuses for his behavior. Maybe he was just too tired, but this morning at breakfast he had completely ignored her and then gone off to work to do the same all day.

Later in the day, his mood seemed to change yet again, and it was as if he was angry with her over something. She couldn't fathom what it might possibly be that she had done that angered him, but he kept his distance the rest of the day and that evening, too.

The next day was a repeat of the afternoon before with his indifference bordering on anger towards her. She tried to ask him what was going on, what she had done, but he ignored her and walked away as if she was invisible.

To say his attitude toward her hurt was an understatement. She was downright heartbroken over it. She had no idea what she had done or why everything had changed between them, so she had no way of knowing how to fix it.

The idea that the rest of her life would drag on like this wasn't even imaginable to her. *What am I going to do? How can I possibly find out what is wrong and go about making it right?*

SEVERAL WEEKS LATER, things had not improved at all between Addie and Boyd. She tried her hardest to please him, to draw him into conversation. She had even spent one week fixing all of his favorite meals for supper each night that week. Nothing had changed. He continued to remain aloof during the day, sometimes bordering on rudeness toward her. At night, he continued to stay away from her.

Finally, in desperation, she hatched a plan to try to seduce him to get him back to her bed. Tonight was the night she had it planned for. She was so nervous she could hardly concentrate on her work. Several different customers had to bring her back into the conversation they had been having about some need or another of theirs.

Mrs. Dewberry gave a delicate cough, bringing her around once more to the customer in front of her. "I'm sorry, Mrs. Dewberry, what did you ask?"

"I asked when that blue calico I ordered last week might be in. I had understood it would arrive today."

"Of course, just let me get to the order ledger, and I'll look that up for you." Addie moved behind the counter and pulled out the order ledger.

After scanning it for Mrs. Dewberry's order, she looked up as she closed the book. "There was a bit of delay due to weather. It looks like it should arrive on tomorrow's freight wagon from Denver."

Mrs. Dewberry gave a nod. "Thank you for the information, Mrs. Larson. I shall return tomorrow afternoon then. Good day."

"Thank you, Mrs. Dewberry. I'll see you tomorrow." She gave a wave to the departing woman, glad she had been able to appease her so easily. The woman could be such a harridan, Addie never knew when she might accidentally incur the woman's ire.

The rest of the afternoon dragged on. Addie wondered if the day would ever end so she could put her plan into action. The more the day wore on, the more anxious she became until she was a nervous wreck when they finally closed the store and went upstairs to their apartment.

As a result of her tension, she burned the special dinner she was making for him from the recipe book he had ordered from a vendor just for her since her cooking skills were atrocious. They had not improved much since then, and nothing seemed to be going right tonight.

Tears were threatening by the time she got the dishes cleaned up and went to their bedroom to get ready for the night. She donned the fanciest flannel gown she owned, one with a pink bow and lace around the neck and sleeves.

She brushed her flowing red locks until they glowed in the dim light given off by the gas lamp. After pinching her cheeks to give them a bit of color, she went so far as to even dab a little of her precious rosewater on.

When she heard Boyd's footsteps coming towards their door, she sprang to the bed and quickly struck a pose that she hoped was seductive.

Addie watched as Boyd entered their room, his eyes darting to the bed and then away just as quickly. He did not speak to her, turning his back on her as he sat down on the edge of the bed to take off his shoes.

This was not going as planned. She had hoped one look at her seductive pose after so many nights without making love would make him come eagerly into her arms again. She should have gone with her first instinct and posed on the bed minus her nightgown, but she had been too shy to do that.

Now, she was glad she had kept her nightgown on. It was humiliating enough for him to completely ignore her, but at least she was decently clothed in her embarrassment.

She scooted closer to Boyd and put her hands to his shoulders to rub his tense-looking muscles. She jerked them away when he visibly flinched at her touch and jumped to his feet, his shoes still on.

To her further humiliation, tears sprang to her eyes about the same time he turned to face her. She did not want him to see her cry, so she turned away.

"Go to sleep, Addie. Tomorrow will be a long day with the freight wagon coming."

The sound of the door opening had her turning in time to see Boyd's retreating back before the door shut firmly behind him. After that, the tears fell freely as she sobbed into her pillow.

CHAPTER 13

Boyd lay awake for a long time on the sofa in the parlor of their apartment thinking about Addie. If he didn't know better, he would say she had been trying to seduce him tonight, but he shoved that thought aside. That didn't sound like Addie to him.

Still, the hurt expression on her face when he had ignored her and left gnawed at his gut. He hated to hurt her, but he couldn't risk getting close to her and deepening the feelings that she had started to awaken.

Again, he wished he'd let the detective know that Addie was there. But why the sudden interest her father had in his daughter after practically throwing her out, Boyd had no idea. Unless it was as he thought before, perhaps she had just said that so he wouldn't send her home when she first arrived.

The calling card the detective had given him had his information on it. If he wanted to, he could simply telegraph the detective and tell him the truth, that Addie is here. But something had kept him from doing it. He didn't want to hurt Addie that much by sending her away.

The truth needed to come out, though, whether she had tricked him or not with her story about her father. Maybe he would dig the card out and send a telegram tomorrow.

The next day at the mercantile the freight wagon arrived earlier than usual, throwing Boyd's whole routine off, and thoughts of contacting the detective were pushed out of his mind as he dealt with the delivery and the problems it brought with it.

He had to admit, though, that he was glad he was busy as he didn't have so much time to dwell on Addie and the dilemma he was having over her. It made it easier to keep her at arm's length when they were both busy with different tasks or helping various customers.

When he chanced a glance at her while helping unload the freight wagon, she was checking the arriving inventory off the order list. It was one of her favorite jobs. She loved it when the deliveries came. Today, her usual smile was missing, and her eyes weren't sparkling like normal.

A flash of guilt stabbed at his conscience that it was his fault she had lost her luster today, but he pushed it aside as he hefted a heavy box off the wagon. He found that if he kept thinking she might have duped him he could keep the guilty feelings at bay.

LATER, BOYD NOTICED Addie and Mrs. Dewberry deep in conversation. He hoped there wasn't a problem with her order. Of all the customers he tried to please the hardest, it was that woman because she was so particular about everything and was a bit of a tyrant, in his opinion.

Surprise shot through him moments later when he saw Mrs. Dewberry's arm go around Addie in what looked like a comforting gesture. He never would have expected that from Mrs. Dewberry!

He wondered if the woman had gotten cross with Addie and upset her. He hoped Mrs. Dewberry's order had arrived and was to her satisfaction. Perhaps that had something to do with Addie's tear-streaked face when she pulled away from the elderly woman.

With a mental note to ask Addie about it later to ensure everything was okay with the woman's order, Boyd went back to work helping to unload the freight wagon.

ADDIE WAS HAVING A hard time keeping her composure that day after her miserable failure at seducing her husband the night before. She heaved a great sigh when the freight wagon arrived with Mrs. Dewberry hot on its trail.

The woman swept into the room on the heels of the freight master and rushed to Addie's side. "Mrs. Larson, did my order arrive?"

With what she hoped was a pleasant smile, Addie turned to the woman. "Good morning, Mrs. Dewberry. The freighter has only just arrived seconds before you." Addie pointed out the obvious fact to the woman in a gentle voice. "I have not had a chance to check over the list of the inventory ordered to indeed verify that it has all arrived."

The elderly woman peered intently at her and then laid her hand on Addie's arm. "Are you feeling well, my dear? You look a bit peaked."

At the woman's unexpected kindness and much to her own horror, Addie burst into tears.

Mrs. Dewberry at once slipped an arm around her and held her, patting her back in a comforting gesture as she cried. "There, there now, dear. What's this all about?"

Addie only cried harder.

The woman led her to a quiet corner in the back of the store where they could talk without being overheard.

"Tell me what's wrong. It will help to get it off your chest."

"Oh, Mrs. Dewberry, my husband can't stand to be around me, and I don't know what to do." More tears burst forth after her confession.

"Now, now, it can't be as bad as all that."

"Oh, but it is. He has gotten to where he will not even stay in the same room with me if he doesn't have to. He completely avoids me."

"Perhaps he has a lot on his mind. From what I have seen, your husband seems quite fond of you. I would even go so far as to say he loves you."

Addie shook her head. "No, he does not love me. He is still in love with his first wife."

"His first wife is dead," Mrs. Dewberry pointed out.

"Yes, I know, but he's still in love with her. He won't even give me a chance."

Mrs. Dewberry shook her head. "Why is it that men are so pigheaded about love?" She patted Addie's back. "Well, we will just have to do something about that."

Addie pulled back and wiped at her tears. "What do you mean?"

"I mean, dear child, that we will need to come up with a plan for you to be so irresistible that he will not be able to ignore you."

With a shake of her head, Addie explained her attempt at seducing her husband and his reaction to it. "You see, it is hopeless. He wants nothing to do with me." In the back of her mind, Addie was having a hard time believing that she was carrying on this conversation with anyone, let alone Mrs. Dewberry.

"You let me think about this for a bit. I'll come up with a plan of some kind," the woman assured her.

CHAPTER 14

Two men who had entered the store moments before came hurrying toward them. "Addie, it is you!"

At the familiar voice calling her name, Addie looked up and was shocked to see her father and another man striding toward her. "Papa?"

When he reached his daughter, Mr. Montgomery threw his arms around her. "Addie, my child. I finally found you."

Addie hugged her father then pulled away and looked him over. He was pale and somewhat gaunt as if he had lost a considerable amount of weight recently. "What do you mean, you finally found me?"

"I have been looking for you for months. I was afraid I was never going to find you, but then my detective, Ed here, told me he may have found you." He indicated the man who had entered with him. "I had to come right away to see for myself if it was you or not."

None of this made any sense to Addie. She gave a shake of her head as she looked at the man her father referred to. It took her a moment to recognize him as the man who had come in about a month earlier and spoken to Boyd. He had given her a good looking-over before he had left. "I don't understand."

Next to her, Mrs. Dewberry cleared her throat.

"Oh, I'm so sorry. Mrs. Dewberry, please meet my father, Mr. Harvey Montgomery. Papa, this is Mrs. Dewberry. She is here to pick up an order that was due to arrive today. Please excuse me, Papa. I need to take care of my customer first but then we need to talk."

"Of course, my dear," Mr. Montgomery said after bowing politely to Mrs. Dewberry.

"Oh, no, Mrs. Larson. My order can wait. You evidently have not seen your father in quite some time and have things to discuss. Perhaps you all would like to go over to the café and have a bite to eat while you have your discussion," Mrs. Dewberry suggested.

"That sounds like a grand idea. What do you say, Addie, can you come with us for a bit?" her father asked.

Looking around for Boyd, Addie was not sure how to answer. The freight wagon had just come and there was much to be done. She really could not leave Boyd by himself to complete the work. "I need to check with my husband first and see if it is alright for me to go."

Mrs. Dewberry waved her away. "You three go on over to the café. I will let your husband know where you have gone and why."

Addie nodded her consent and was surprised when her father turned to Mrs. Dewberry. "It would be a pleasure if you would join us after you speak to him."

"Thank you, Mr. Montgomery. I would enjoy that."

Surprised by her father's invitation to the woman, Addie looked at Mrs. Dewberry and was amazed to see that she was blushing when she answered. *Hmmm, I wonder what that means?* Slipping her arm into her father's, the two of them and the detective left the store.

Outside, Addie's father took a few moments to speak to the detective alone. When they were finished, the man tipped his hat to Addie and took his leave as her father rejoined her on the boardwalk.

CHAPTER 15

Once the two were seated at the café, Addie turned to her father. "What are you doing here? I thought you did not want to see me any longer."

"Is that what Esther told you? No wonder you did not tell me that you were leaving. I have been looking everywhere. I started searching the minute I realized what was happening."

"What do you mean realized what was happening? I thought you didn't love me any longer now that Mama died."

"Oh, my sweet girl. You are my pride and joy. I will always love you. Esther did a fine job of making you believe that I no longer did, didn't she?"

Addie threw her arms around her father. "Oh Papa, you don't know how glad I am to hear that! I've missed you so."

"You need never doubt that again. I will always love you, Addie."

"I don't understand, though. What happened once I left?"

Her father shifted in his chair, his face turning red. He cleared his throat a time or two before speaking. "I do not know what I was thinking when I married Esther. In fact, I suspect that she may have drugged me somehow, but it could have just been my grief that got me into that mess."

"Oh, Papa, you don't think she would really drug you, do you?"

"You have not heard the whole story yet, child."

At that moment, the waitress came over to take their orders. Since neither had bothered to look at the small menu on the table, they both ordered the special of roast beef with potatoes, carrots, gravy, and a roll.

Once the waitress left, Mr. Montgomery continued his story. "I had taken ill not too long after I married Esther. Thinking it was just because

I had not been taking care of myself in my grief, I thought I would return to health with Esther there cooking and caring for me."

"I didn't realize you were ill."

"You were grieving for your mother, and I did not want to give you another burden, so I kept it from you. But instead of getting better, I seemed to get worse. I wondered why you never came to see me once I was too ill to get out of bed..."

"Esther told me you were grieving for Mama so badly that you wouldn't come out of your study. I accepted her story because I knew how deeply it had hurt you when Mama died."

Her father shook his head. "Why did you leave, Addie?"

Addie looked down at her hands. "Esther told me that you missed Mama so much and I reminded you too much of her, so you wanted me to leave."

"And you believed her?" Her father's eyebrows shot up in disbelief.

"What was I supposed to think when she had told me that you were grieving too much to come out of your study?"

"Well, I suppose you're right. That woman was good at weaving her lies. After a while, I began to suspect that maybe Esther was poisoning me, so I ate as little as I could for a few days to get my strength back up. Then I went out one day while Esther was away and went to see the doctor. After hearing my story and examining me, he believed the same thing."

Addie's hand flew to her mouth. "Oh, Papa, no! I never suspected that Esther was evil enough to do that. What did you do after that?"

"Esther must have gotten wind or suspected where I had gone when she returned home that day because when I got home with the sheriff in tow, she and all her things were gone. It's a good thing she didn't have the combination to my office safe. She didn't know I had valuables there, including some of the jewelry that belonged to your mama."

"So, she got away with trying to kill you?"

Mr. Montgomery nodded. "For now, anyway. The police did some checking on her, though, and apparently her first husband died of mysterious circumstances back in New York before she moved to Chicago."

Flinging her arms around her father, Addie cried against his chest. "Oh, Papa, I almost lost you for good. I'm so sorry I doubted you."

Her father patted her back. "It is understandable, child."

The waitress appeared with their meals, so Addie broke away from her father and wiped her eyes.

They both dug into their meals and were quiet for several minutes as they ate. Finally, stabbing a piece of meat with his fork, Mr. Montgomery said, "Tell me how you came to live here and about your husband. How did you meet him?"

Addie looked down at her plate. "After Esther told me that you no longer wanted me there, she gave me newspapers from several different cities and told me to look through them for somewhere to go. I found an advertisement from Mr. Larson, Boyd, for a mail-order bride. I wrote back and he asked me to come west to marry him. Since I thought I had no other option, I accepted."

Her father had laid down his fork while she spoke and stared at her in shock. "You traveled west and married a complete stranger?"

Addie looked up at her father. "I had no choice, Papa. Besides, Boyd is a kind man."

"So, he is an extremely kind man?"

"Yes, Papa."

"Then why were you crying when I entered the mercantile?"

It was Addie's turn to look surprised. "You noticed that?"

"Your face was tear-streaked when I approached you," he explained.

Addie took another bite of her meal and tried to decide how to explain the situation to her father as she chewed. When she swallowed, she said, "It is complicated. Boyd was married previously, and he lost his wife to illness. He has closed off his emotions, and he does not love me."

Her father studied her for a moment. "But you love him?"

She nodded. "I have come to love him very much, but it is difficult to live with someone when they do not love you back."

"I see." Her father looked deep in thought as he took another bite.

"I am not sure what to do. I do not know how much longer I can go on this way without him loving me. It is just too hard."

After a few more bites, Mr. Montgomery said, "I'll be staying here for a few days, but then I will need to return home. You can always come back home with me."

"I don't know if I want to do that, either."

"Well, think about it, and you can let me know before I leave."

Addie nodded. "I will think about it and make a decision before you go."

At that moment, Mrs. Dewberry entered the café and made her way over to their table.

Mr. Montgomery stood and pulled out an empty chair for her to sit.

Addie saw Mrs. Dewberry blushing as her father took his seat next to her. *Hmm, I wonder what that is all about? Mrs. Dewberry sure has been a surprise today!*

CHAPTER 16

The freight wagon was finally unloaded, and the freighter had gone on his way. Boyd had checked the inventory against the order with the freighter since Addie had gone to the café. There was still much to be done putting away the order, but he found it hard to concentrate with his conversation with Mrs. Dewberry running through his mind.

"Mr. Larson, what exactly are you up to?"

Mrs. Dewberry's question had taken him by surprise when she had confronted him inside the mercantile just after he had deposited a load from the freight wagon on the floor near the counter.

Taken aback by her abrupt question, he stated the obvious. "I'm unloading the freight wagon. Is there something wrong with your order?"

"I do not give a lick about my order. I want to know what it is you think you are doing with your wife?" She jabbed her finger into his chest.

"My wife? I saw you speaking to her earlier. She must still be about somewhere," he said, still unsure what Mrs. Dewberry was upset with him about.

"Your wife has gone to the café to visit with her father. That is right," she said when he raised his eyebrows questioningly at her. "With her father, the same father who sent a detective looking for her...the same detective that you told you had never heard of anyone by that name."

"How do you know all this?" Boyd asked, feeling himself flush guiltily at being caught in his lie to the detective.

"I was there when her father and the detective showed up. I told them to go visit at the café, and I would settle things with you about Addie leaving. But that's really not what I was referring to."

Boyd shook his head. "I am sorry, Mrs. Dewberry, I really do not know what you are talking about then. I did tell the detective that because Addie told me that her father wanted nothing to do with her once her mother died, so I felt if she did not want him to know where she was then I had no right to disclose that to the detective."

"Well, it was honorable for you to stick up for your wife, but like I said, I was not referring to that. I want to know why you have a beautiful wife like you do and then refuse to love her because of your deceased wife."

When he said nothing, she continued her tirade. "Your previous wife, God rest her soul, is gone. You cannot bring her back. You need to live your life. She would not have wanted you to be this way after her death. She would want you to find someone else to care for and to care for you."

After taking a deep breath, she went on. "You brought that young lady here from her home in the east and married her. Now, you need to decide whether you want to keep her or not because she is mighty unhappy. Now that her father is here, I would not be surprised if she returned East with him when he goes."

Speechless, Boyd could say nothing. He just stared at the woman with that guilty flush on his face, feeling like it was getting darker and darker.

"Now, I am going to join Mrs. Larson and Mr. Montgomery at the café. I will tell your wife that you have given her the rest of the day off to visit with her father...and *you* need to think about what I said and what you intend to do about the mess you have made." With that, she had turned and stomped from the shop.

Now that she was gone and Boyd needed to get busy, he could not stop thinking about what she had said. *Would Addie really go back to Chicago with her father? Why am I worried about it? It's what would be best. It's what I want, isn't it?*

Dragging himself away from where Mrs. Dewberry had left him standing, Boyd forced himself to get busy unpacking the order and putting it away. He had forgotten how long it took for just him to do it, and he missed Addie's company while he worked. *Do I really want her to leave? This is what it will be like again if she does.*

BOYD HAD GIVEN ADDIE time off to spend with her father while he was in town. She surprised him when she packed a carryall and went to stay with her father in his suite of rooms at the hotel.

With Addie gone, the next several days dragged by for Boyd as he worked in the mercantile alone. It was a chance for him to see what it would be like with Addie gone. He did not like it. He wondered if she was planning on coming back home when her father left, even though she had told him it was only while her father was in town. Still, he wondered why she wouldn't return to Chicago with her father, since he had been so cold toward her.

As he worked, Boyd would find himself missing her at the oddest times. His mind and emotions were in turmoil. It would be easier on him in so many ways if she were to return home with her father. Yet, in so many other ways, it would be horrible if she did.

Well, now he knew the details about her coming here and that she had not duped him after all. Mrs. Dewberry had told him the whole story once she had learned it. Addie barely spoke to him before she left. She spent most of her time with her father.

CHAPTER 17

Surprisingly, Mrs. Dewberry was spending quite a bit of time with Addie and her father, also. He wondered what that was all about. *Is she keeping tabs on them to report back to me? She is the reason I know what is going on.* That did not seem likely.

He wondered if Mrs. Dewberry and Mr. Montgomery were attracted to each other. Evidently, Mr. Montgomery was alone now and had been since not long after Addie left. Mrs. Dewberry had been alone for a long time. She deserved to find someone to spend her golden years with.

Boyd was just glad Addie had not tricked him, but it was easier to push away his feelings for her when he thought she might have. Now, thoughts and memories of her overwhelmed him throughout the day, causing him to miss her. The nights were worse. It was then that he yearned for her. Their pillows carried her scent, which sent memories of their good nights together racing through his imagination. When he found a strand of red hair on one of his shirts, he wound it around his finger and put it in an envelope. At least he'd have that tiny thing to remind him of what he'd lost.

If he did happen to be lucky enough to get to sleep, he was inevitably awakened by dreams of her.

It was driving him crazy, and she had only been gone two days. Tonight, would be the third night. He had not gotten much sleep the past two nights without Addie. Her father had the rest of her things delivered to the hotel the previous night. Boyd was afraid she was going to leave. *How am I going to stand it?* Sucking in a deep breath, he pushed thoughts of her away and tried to concentrate on updating the sales ledger.

Before long, the numbers blurred, and visions of Addie danced before his eyes. With a sigh, he brushed his hand wearily down his face. *This is not getting me anywhere.* Pulling out his pocket watch, he noted it was after six o'clock. *Thank goodness. I thought this day would never end.* With a sigh of relief, Boyd went to turn the sign on the front door and turn the lock.

With a flick of his fingers, he flipped the sign from Open to Closed and reached out to lock the door when it flew open.

Mrs. Dewberry strode in, giving him an appraising look.

"I was just locking up," he said, wondering if she had finally remembered her order from the other day that she still needed to pick up.

She waved a hand toward the door. "By all means, go ahead and lock up. I am not here to conduct business."

Tired and reluctant to speak to anyone at the moment, Boyd slowly locked the door then turned to face his visitor. "What can I do for you this evening, Mrs. Dewberry?"

Putting her hands on her hips, the woman gave him a stern look. "It is not what you can do for me, Mr. Larson. I want to know what you intend to do about your wife?"

He scrubbed a hand across his face. "I'm sorry?"

"Your lovely wife is planning to leave tomorrow with her father to return to Chicago. What do you plan on doing about it? That is all I was wondering. Now, if you will excuse me, I am dining with your wife and her father this evening." With that, she strode back to the door and waited for him to unlock it, apparently not wanting a reply from him.

There was no way he could have replied, even if he had wanted to. His throat had tightened with the news of Addie's impending departure, so he did not think he could squeeze any words past it. This was the first he heard about Addie returning to Chicago with her father. He wondered if she planned on telling him goodbye. Why would she want to?

After locking back up after Mrs. Dewberry, Boyd went through the back room and climbed the stairs to the apartment with a heavy step that matched his heavy heart. Not only had Mrs. Dewberry's news taken him by surprise, but it saddened him, too. Memories of his and Addie's time together crowded his mind. When he recalled his treatment of her recently, a wave of shame washed over him. *Did I really expect her to stay after the way I have treated her?*

His appetite had retreated the day Addie left, but he snagged an apple out of the bowl on the table and forced himself to take a bite of it. It might as well have been made of mud, for all he tasted it. He moved to his chair in the parlor and sat down, putting his feet up on the stool.

Mrs. Dewberry had a good question. *What am I going to do about Addie?* The reason he did not want to fall in love with Addie in the first place, his late wife flitted through his mind. He closed his eyes, trying to picture Mary's face but came up blank. Instead, Addie's image swam behind his eyelids.

CHAPTER 18

At dinner with her father and Mrs. Dewberry, Addie tried to follow the conversation, but thoughts of Boyd kept distracting her from what was being said. *Why has he not even tried to see me the past few days? He let me leave like it meant nothing to him. Will he even try to stop me from leaving for ho...Chicago tomorrow?*

She could not seem to make herself say home any longer when referencing Chicago. After living in Leadville for the past five or six months, she had fallen in love with it, and it had become home to her. *How can I bear to leave here? How can I bear to leave Boyd? I will be a disgrace back in Chicago if I seek a divorce. Oh, what am I going to do? Why could he not love me as I love him? How can I stay and face a life of loneliness?*

Lost in thought, it was several moments before Addie realized her father and Mrs. Dewberry had donned their jackets and were standing, waiting for her to rise.

Her father searched her face. "Are you alright, Addie?"

"I am fine, Papa, perhaps just tired."

"I am going to walk Mrs. Dewberry home. Why don't you go on up to the suite? You can finish your packing and get some rest. It's a long journey."

"Papa, don't you need to pack, too?"

"I didn't pack much," he said. "You might want to let your husband know you plan to leave him."

"He won't care." Addie choked on tears she didn't want to shed.

"I'll be back shortly."

Addie nodded. "Yes, Papa." She turned to Mrs. Dewberry. "Goodnight, Mrs. Dewberry. Thank you for everything."

Mrs. Dewberry took her hands and gave them a squeeze. "I shall be here in the morning to see you off."

Her father gave her a peck on the cheek then turned to Mrs. Dewberry. "Are you ready, Myra?"

Mrs. Dewberry blushed a becoming shade of pink and nodded. "Yes, thank you, Harvey." She slipped her arm into the one he offered to her, and they took off.

Addie stood, staring after them until they disappeared through the door. *When did those two become close enough to be on a given-name basis?*

"Did you need anything else, ma'am?"

The waitress's question brought Addie out of her shock. "No, thank you." She turned and left, but as she walked up the stairway to the rooms above, she could not help dwelling over the fact that her father and Mrs. Dewberry were getting so friendly. She was not sure how she felt about that after dealing with Esther.

The hope in Addie's heart that she had awoken with the next morning fled completely by the time she boarded the stagecoach. Mrs. Dewberry came to see her and her father off, but Boyd did not show up. After saying goodbye to Mrs. Dewberry, Addie climbed the steps, leaving her father to say his goodbye to Mrs. Dewberry in private.

Addie's chest squeezed tightly as she took a seat on the hard bench. *Why did Boyd not come and ask me to stay? Do I mean nothing to him at all?* In an effort to squelch the tears that were threatening, she stared at the ceiling, blinking rapidly several times. Unable to bear the pain, she laid her head back against the seat and closed her eyes.

A few minutes later, someone sat down next to her. Assuming it was her father, she kept her eyes closed, not wishing to speak to him just yet. Seconds later, they popped open when someone took her hand and she found herself staring at her husband, his gaze intent.

"Addie, please don't go. I have been miserable since you left."

Her eyes locked with his, Addie could make no reply. She had given up hope that he would come. But she had already decided that she would be firm in her resolve if he did show up unless he included a declaration of love.

His smile slipped somewhat. He squeezed her hand. "Please, Addie. I have been such a fool. I love you with every fiber of my being, and I do not want to live without you. Will you please stay and grow old with me?"

Heart pounding wildly in her chest and tears welling in her eyes, Addie broke into a smile. Still unable to find her voice, she nodded and flung her arms around him. His arms encircled her, and they held each other until the sound of a man clearing his throat broke them apart.

Addie felt her face heat as she looked up at her father.

"I take it you will not be joining me on the journey, after all," he said with a smile.

Finally finding her voice, Addie said, "No, Papa. I shall remain here with my husband." Tears welled in her eyes once more. "But I hate to see you leave."

With a pat on her shoulder, he said, "It will not be for long. I had hoped you would decide to stay as I have found myself fond of this town. I decided that if you chose to stay, I would return home to settle things there before coming back here to live."

Getting to her feet, tears pouring down her face, Addie threw her arms around her father. "That makes me so happy, Papa. I shall have the two men I love here with me."

After Addie kissed her father goodbye, the two men shook hands.

"Have a safe trip. We will see you soon," Boyd said, turning to escort Addie out the door and down the steps. "Unload my wife's trunk, please!" He called to the stagecoach driver.

EPILOGUE

By the time July Fourth rolled around, Addie's father had been living in Leadville for almost a month. He and Mrs. Dewberry had been spending a lot of time together since his return. They were seated with Addie and Boyd on a blanket spread out on the boardwalk. Dusk was approaching and Addie was excited to view the fireworks with both her husband and her father.

The day had been wonderful. It had started that morning with a parade down Harrison Avenue, the main thoroughfare of town, and then there was a picnic. After everyone had topped off their meal with ice cream, the games and races began. Addie's favorite had been the hose cart race put on by the local fire volunteers. Boyd had taken part, and she had enjoyed watching her handsome husband racing down the road as he and his fellow firemen pulled the cart behind them as fast as they could go. She was thrilled when they won first prize.

With a contented sigh, Addie laid her head on Boyd's shoulder, hugging his arm to her as they waited for the evening entertainment. She was so happy that she had not given up on her marriage and returned to Chicago. Now, she found it hard to believe that she had given up faith in both her husband's and father's love for her. She did not know how she could have doubted them. Both of them, as well as Mrs. Dewberry, had been overjoyed when she had announced earlier today that she was expecting sometime in December. Smiling, she remembered it and happiness bubbled up inside her.

Tilting her head up, she gazed at Boyd's handsome countenance. His steady blue gaze settled on hers, sending sparks flying between them.

"I love you, Addie. I am so happy I could burst." He slowly lowered his mouth to hers just as a big boom sounded and the first fireworks lit the sky in a brilliant cascade of red, white, and blue.

CONNECT WITH THE AUTHOR/PUBLISHER:
Join the Kayler Rose Publishing social media sites!
X
https://twitter.com/KaylerRosePub
Facebook
https://www.facebook.com/KaylerRosePublishing

About the Author

Rhiana Rhiley grew up watching Westerns on TV and was raised in the West, so she has a natural love of all things Western. She still loves watching the old westerns today, as well as reading and writing Western romances.

For someone who loved to create her own characters and write her own stories, writing Westerns was a natural progression. Rhiana writes Western romance because she believes in true love and a happy ending for everyone.

Rhiana lives in Western Colorado with her husband and two cats.

www.ingramcontent.com/pod-product-compliance
Lightning Source LLC
Chambersburg PA
CBHW030238180626
46810CB00008B/3187